CREPE EXPECTATIONS

CROOKED BAY COZY MYSTERIES, BOOK 1

PATTI BENNING

SUMMER PRESCOTT BOOKS PUBLISHING

CHAPTER ONE

It felt good to slam the front door behind her, even though a decade ago she would have taken her son to task about doing the same thing. It was petty, but there was no one else in the house for the noise to bother, and it helped her feel better, just a little bit. That was as much as she could hope for these days.

She dropped her purse on the side table and unclipped the name tag from her shirt with a wrench, tossing the plastic card that read *Theresa Tremblay* in the same general direction. The photo on the card showed a happier version of herself and had been taken five years earlier, before her deep brown hair started to turn grey at the temples and her blue eyes turned sad. She didn't pause to look where it had landed—she was *done*.

For the day, at least. While she loved to fantasize about standing up at her desk in the middle of the workday and telling her boss she quit, a fantasy was all it was. She had worked payroll in the same office since she was twenty-five—two decades, now. She would probably work there until she retired. When she thought of the fact that she was only halfway through her working life at the place, the future seemed to spiral out in front of her in shades of depressing gray, so she tried not to think about it very often.

Theresa entered the kitchen and started the kettle. She always felt this way after work: frustrated, trapped, dull. It would fade once she got a chance to drink her tea and sit down in her favorite armchair with a good book, only to return when her alarm went off the next morning. She hadn't minded the job so much when Nicolas was still here; then, life had been more than just work, sleep, and repeat. There had been light and laughter and something to look forward to other than retirement twenty years off. Then he died, and it seemed like most of what had made her life so bright, died with him.

She missed her husband.

Once the water boiled, she poured it over a teabag and carried the mug into the living room. She settled into her recliner, kicked her feet up, and sighed. It was good to be home, but already she felt the stresses of the next day creeping up on her. Maybe a vacation was what she needed. Maybe she should take some time off and go visit her parents in Florida.

Her cell phone rang. It was still in her purse, which meant she had to push the old recliner's persnickety footrest down, set her tea on the table next to the chair, and walk all the way back to the front door to get it. It was a miracle that she made it in time, but when she saw whose name was on the caller ID, she almost wished she hadn't.

Clare Bardot. Her cousin. If there was a black sheep in their family, it was Clare. Theresa had bailed the younger woman out of trouble more than once. She was almost tempted not to answer the call since she was already at the end of her rope today, but Clare was family. Theresa wasn't about to ignore her family, even if the family member in question still owed her two thousand dollars from the last time she'd gotten in over her head.

"Hello?" Hopefully, Clare wouldn't notice how wary her greeting sounded.

"Terra! I'm glad you answered. For a second, I thought the call was going to go to voicemail."

"Is there an emergency?" She wondered if she had

jinxed herself by thinking how much she hated her drab and dreary life. She would take drab and dreary over a family emergency any day.

"No, no, nothing like that," Clare said, to Theresa's relief. "But still, there's no time to waste. I found the *perfect* place for you."

"What are you talking about?" Her concern had changed to befuddlement. She hadn't talked to Clare for a few weeks and wondered if she was out of the loop on something essential.

"Remember how you used to talk about opening a crêpe restaurant?"

"A crêperie?" Theresa laughed. "Sure, when I was twenty. How do you even remember that? You would have been, what, ten at the time?"

"You told me while you taught me how to make crêpes, of course I remember it. Those were very good crêpes. Besides, Nick always said he thought you should open your own restaurant. Don't you remember?"

Of course she did. She was hardly going to forget her own husband's compliments towards her cooking. But that was all they were: compliments. Sweet nothings any husband would say.

"Well, regardless, what does my cooking have to

with anything?" she asked, steering the conversation away from him.

"Like I said, I found the perfect place for you. For your restaurant. It's right here in Crooked Bay. The place came up for sale last week, and I finally got around to looking it up. The price is unbeatable, Terra. And it's an adorable little building. You can see the bay if you step out onto Lake Street. It would be perfect for you."

"Clare, I appreciate it, but opening a restaurant was only ever a dream. And a young person's dream, at that."

"Don't you want to at least hear the price?"

Theresa sighed. "Fine. Go ahead."

Clare told her, and despite herself, Theresa felt a spark of interest. Somehow, her cousin must have sensed it, because she said, "I told you; it's a great deal."

"That's beyond a great deal. There must be something wrong with the place, for that price." Her cousin's silence told her all she needed to know. "Clare?"

"Well, the last owner—or maybe they were renting it, I don't know—*might* have been murdered inside the building. But they caught the guy who did it! The price is just low because everyone around town knows the story, and you know how small-town people can be. They probably think it's haunted or something."

"Look, Clare, I really appreciate you calling me." She did—she felt better, at least. Chatting with her cousin had chased that flat, dull feeling her job left her with away for now. "But I'm not looking to open a crêperie, let alone move halfway across the state to do it. It would be fun if I was younger, if—" *If Nicolas was still here.* "If things were different. But they're not."

"The two of you always talked about moving closer to one of the Great Lakes," Clare said. "And I know you like Crooked Bay. You two used to come up here every summer. Are you really happy right now, Terra? Don't you want a change?"

"I'm not leaving my home, Clare," she said. It was the house she and Nicolas had worked so hard to get just the way they liked it. She hadn't changed a thing since he passed. "I'll try to take the time to visit this summer, but opening a restaurant, uprooting my life… I'm too settled for that. I'm … content where I am."

It was a lie, and it tasted sour on her tongue, but she refused to let anyone in her family know how miserable she truly was.

"Well, that's too bad," Clare said. She didn't *sound* disappointed; if anything, she sounded smug, which set off alarm bells for Theresa. "Because I already sent Jace the listing and mentioned just how cute a little crêpe shop would be there."

"Clare—"

Her cousin hung up, but Theresa knew the damage was done. As if the end of the call had summoned them, her phone started buzzing with incoming text messages, all from her son. The first one was the online listing for the building, and the others were various versions of, *This is such a great idea, Mom. You've got to do it.*

Theresa did something she rarely did and ignored her son. She still read all his messages, of course, just in case something important came up, but decided not to respond until he'd had a chance to step back and realize how insane this idea really was. Her tea was lukewarm when she got back to it, and she had a hard time focusing on her book, but for the most part, she was successful in pushing the craziness her cousin and her son had involved themselves in aside.

Until someone knocked at her door. That was such a rare occurrence these days, when everyone called first, that she approached the door with a certain wariness, already planning how to politely tell whoever was on the other side that she didn't want what they were selling.

Her words died on her tongue when she opened the door to see her son standing on the porch.

"Jace, what are you doing here? You didn't tell me you were coming over."

"I had a feeling you'd pretend you were busy if I asked," he said, raising his eyebrows. "Can I come in?"

"Of course." She stepped aside and pulled him into a quick hug once he was through the door, still glad she could do that again. He'd gone through a phase during his teenage years where he acted like any sort of affection from either of his parents burned him like acid. That had changed after Nicolas's death, along with everything else. She was just glad Jace seemed to have adjusted to it better than she was; he was twenty-two, a fresh college graduate, and had so much to look forward to.

"Layla asked me to tell you hi."

"Oh. Well, tell her I say hi back." Layla was Jace's long-term girlfriend. Theresa liked her, she supposed. She seemed like a nice girl, and a good fit to Jace, but sometimes she felt like they came from different worlds. "Is she working?"

"No, she's off today, but I wanted to talk just the

two of us."

She rarely heard such serious words come out of her son's mouth and wondered if she had somehow missed an important text. "Is everything all right?"

He gave her a strange, sad smile and ushered her into the living room. She sat down stiffly on the armchair, feeling her heart beat too hard in her chest. Why wasn't he answering?

"That's what I wanted to ask you, Mom."

"What?"

"You're not happy."

"I … I am. Of course I am. Well, with your father gone, it's hard—" She faltered. She didn't want to lie to her son, but she didn't want to tell him the truth either. "Why are you here? Is it just because I wasn't answering your messages earlier?"

"Sort of," he said. "Clare told me about the building for sale—"

"You know how Clare is—"

"Just let me talk, okay, Mom?" He raised an eyebrow. She mimed zipping her lips, and he continued. "She told me about the building for sale, then after she talked to you, she called me back. You didn't even consider it, did you?"

"Of course not," she said. "It's a ridiculous idea."

"It's not. I'm not saying you have to open a crêpe

shop, but I'm worried about you, Mom. Something needs to change."

His words filled her with guilt. The last thing she had ever wanted was to make her son worry about her. "You shouldn't worry, Jace. I'm fine."

"You're not," he said. "When's the last time you took a vacation? Or went out to dinner? Shoot, Mom, you haven't even hung new pictures or bought a new bedspread since Dad died. It's like he died, but you're the one who became a ghost. The two of you used to talk about moving to a little town by the lake or buying a cottage up north. You used to talk about finding a job that felt fulfilling, even if it made less money, once I was out of college. You guys had all these plans, things you were excited for. I don't even remember the last time I saw you smile."

"I smile whenever I see you."

"I don't mean just a smile in greeting. I mean a smile because you're actually happy."

She remained silent. She didn't know what to say to him. He sighed and ran a hand through his short hair.

"It's not like you couldn't afford to move. I'm guessing you still have most of his life insurance money left over, don't you?"

"I haven't touched a penny other than what I set

aside for you."

"Why?"

She looked away, her eyes finding the picture of her and Nicolas on their honeymoon to France on the mantle. "Money can't buy me what I want, Jace."

"I'm not going to tell you to move on or whatever, because I know Dad was the love of your life. But even I can tell you aren't happy. And it's not just that you aren't happy, but you're not *trying* to be happy. It's like you've given up. Do you really think he'd want that for you? He'd want you to take that money and use it to live the life you'd always dreamed of."

"Neither of us know what he'd want. We can't ask him."

"I know because he told me, Mom." Jace held her gaze. "He told me he wanted us both to be happy—he made me promise to try to find joy every day, and I know he wouldn't want any less for you. You've got to at least try, Mom. If you won't do it for yourself or for Dad, do it for me. Do you think I like knowing my mom's so unhappy she barely even smiles when she sees me?"

Theresa swallowed against a lump in her throat. "I didn't know you felt this way, Jace. You're right, I'm not happy, but I don't think that's something moving or starting a business would fix."

"It might be a start, though." He looked around the house. "Come on, Mom, this place is like a shrine. You work in a basement office doing the same thing every single day. It's no wonder you're in a rut."

"So, what, you think I should hare off to Crooked Bay to open a crêperie? Is this my midlife crisis?"

"Honestly?" He cocked an eyebrow. "Why not? Isn't the thought at all exciting? Heck, Mom, you could walk into work tomorrow, tell your boss you quit, and have a completely different life within a month."

For the first time, she ignored the gut reaction that this entire crazy idea was impossible and stopped to actually consider it. She tried to imagine waking up in the morning not to punch numbers under flickering fluorescent lights, but to make food and put smiles on people's faces. She thought about what it would be like to take a walk along Lake Huron's shore after work, to meet people who looked at her as something other than a widow. She wondered how it would feel to be excited about life again.

"You know what, Jace?" She took a deep breath and felt the beginnings of her first real smile in a long time. "I still think this whole thing is crazy. But maybe it's time to be a little crazy. Why not give it a try?"

CHAPTER TWO

In the end, it took almost two months to turn her entire life on its head. She didn't tell her boss she was quitting on the spot at work the next day, but somehow, knowing she wasn't going to be going into that office every day for the next twenty years made her time there more manageable. She gave her two weeks' notice, and on the last day, she almost felt nostalgic for all the years she had spent there. She hugged coworkers she'd barely said ten words to since Nicolas's funeral and had to fight back tears when they told her how much they would miss her.

But that first morning she woke up and didn't have to face going into work felt like the first breath of fresh air she'd had in a long time. Standing inside the small, empty building Clare had told her about and telling the real estate agent she wanted to put an offer in on it felt a lot like that time she and Nicolas had gone cliff diving back in college. It was exhilarating. It was frightening. She just hoped when she hit the waves, she didn't drown.

Once her offer was in, things moved quickly. She listed her house, started apartment shopping in Crooked Bay—she asked Clare to visit the listings for her, since it was a good three-hour drive away—and started the long task of packing up her house. It was an emotional couple of months—she did a lot of crying, more than she would admit to anyone and certainly more than she would ever let Jace know about. A couple of times, she woke up in the dead of night, certain she had made a horrible mistake. Once or twice, she was on the verge of calling the whole thing off, but there was always something that held her back. Hope for the future, and a dream she had forgotten about for over twenty years.

Mostly, it was the determination not to be miserable for the rest of her life.

Before she knew it, the day had come. She had the keys to her new apartment—or rather, Clare did—she had accepted an offer on her house, she had closed on the little building that would soon become the first crêperie in Crooked Bay, and she could no longer put off the start of her new adventure.

Jace and Layla came to help her move. They had rented a big truck, and Jace had somehow convinced a few of his friends from college to come and help. He barely let her lift a finger—she stood back and watched as, box by box, her life was packed away.

When the house was empty, she and Jace stood side by side in the living room, alone. His friends had left, and Layla was waiting in the truck, having already given her a quick hug and telling her she was excited to see the new apartment. Theresa put an arm around her son's shoulders and squeezed.

"Are you sure you're okay with this?"

He turned to look at her like she was insane. "Am *I* okay with this? I'm the one who convinced you to do it, Mom."

"I know, but this is the house you grew up in, sweetie. We both have a lot of memories here." She gave a sad smile. "Good ones."

"I'll miss it," Jace admitted. "But things change. Honestly, ever since Dad died, I've had a hard time coming here. That part of our life is over now. I think it's good that someone else will live in this house and make their own memories in it. This was a good decision, Mom."

"I'm going to miss you." Moving to Crooked Bay meant moving away from her son. He had gone to college not too far away from his childhood home and had gotten an apartment in the area afterward. He lived his own life, but he saw her most weeks, and she would miss that dearly.

"I'll miss you too, but it's not like I was going to stay around here forever. I have leads on a few jobs that look interesting."

"What? Why didn't you tell me sooner? That's so exciting, Jace."

"I'll tell you when I have something solid," he said, laughing. "My point is, don't feel bad. I wouldn't want you to stay here just for me anyway. And I'm going to feel a lot better about moving to another city if I know you're in a better place."

"You'd better not tell your friends I'm in a better place now," she said. "It sounds like I joined your father."

He chuckled. "Bad choice of words," he admitted. "Are you ready to go? It's a bit of a drive. It would be nice to at least be done unpacking the truck before dark. It's going to go a lot slower without my friends to help."

"Thank goodness my apartment's on the ground floor," she said. "You can go ahead and get in the truck if you'd like. In fact, why don't you hit the road? It's all right if you get there before me, Clare will be waiting. I'm going to take a couple minutes here by myself first."

He gave her one last hug and left. She heard the truck start outside and pull away. Taking a deep breath, she slowly turned in place in the empty living room. She felt a lump in her throat. She and Nick had always planned on moving, but she thought this day would come with him by her side. She'd never thought she would be facing this part of her life alone.

"We had good times here," she whispered. "I miss you. I hope I'm making the right choice."

She left through the front door, pausing to drop off the keys in the lockbox for her real estate agent. As she got into her crossover, which was stuffed full of bags of clothing and linens, and pulled out of the driveway, she didn't look back. It was time to move forward.

It was late afternoon by the time she got to Crooked Bay. Jace and Layla had already arrived, and Clare was helping them unload. She was eager to see her new apartment in person for the first time, but her first stop was at the building that would soon be her crêperie. This place, more than the apartment, was her reason for moving here. The apartment was temporary—if this worked out, she would buy a house in the area—but it was likely she would work in this building for the rest of her life.

She parked along the curb. It was the third building down from the intersection of Lake Street and Main Street. It was to the west of the intersection, on the south side of the road, and just like Clare had said, she could see the bay from where she was parked on Lake Street. Beyond the bay, Lake Huron's waters stretched farther than she could see.

Crooked Bay was a tiny town on the eastern coast of Michigan's Lower Peninsula. She had visited the area often, but had never lived on the water before, and was looking forward to being able to go to the beach whenever she wanted. It would be a different sort of life than the one she had led in central Michigan, but then, that was the point, wasn't it?

She got out of her car and walked onto the side-walk, staring up at her building. It was one story, brick, and square. Unlike many of the other buildings in Crooked Bay's small downtown strip, it didn't have an apartment above it. It stood alone, divided from the buildings on either side by narrow alleys. There was a shared parking lot in the back, which was where she would normally park. Today, though, she didn't plan on staying long.

She had the keys in her hand and was about to stride forward and unlock the front door, when she frowned. "It's crooked."

She hadn't noticed it before, but the front door had been set, ever so slightly crooked into the bricks. The entire door was tilted, with one of the top corners higher than the other, and now that she had noticed it, she knew she would never be able to overlook it again.

She stepped back, squinting. Both of the large windows on either side of the door were straight. The walls were straight, the roof was strong. It was just the door that was crooked.

"How odd."

Her inspector hadn't mentioned it, so she decided it probably wasn't important. It was just a small quirk she would have to get used to. It was much better than the building's other quirk—she hadn't forgotten Clare had told her the previous tenant had been murdered inside it.

She unlocked the door and went in. The building had been a coffee shop before, so there was already a kitchen and a sales counter. Almost everything else had been stripped out and sold. She would be starting completely from scratch. That was okay, though. She was dipping into her husband's life insurance money for this. She had ignored the money for the last three years, not wanting to feel as though she was profiting from his death, but she knew she couldn't ignore it forever. She thought he would approve of her using it for this, to follow one of her oldest dreams. Jace was right about that—it seemed her son was right about a lot of things.

She walked around the small, empty building slowly, trailing her fingers over the brick walls. She stepped into the single restroom, explored the narrow back hall that led to a tiny, windowless office that reminded her much of her cubicle at work, and a storage room. The kitchen took up maybe a quarter of the entire building. It was small but not cramped, and had a high ceiling with exposed beams. The windows were set close to the ceiling but still let in plenty of light. It felt artsy, and she thought it was the perfect place to make crêpes. She'd been making them almost every morning since she decided to jump into this feetfirst, experimenting with different toppings and twists on the recipe. It was only after she had made her first batch that she realized she hadn't made crêpes at all since Nicolas's death. That had been another reminder of just how far into a daily rut she had fallen.

"You're perfect," she whispered to the building

when she returned to the main area. It had old wooden floorboards that needed a good polish, but she loved it. Somehow, it already felt like home. "We're going to have quite the adventure together, you and I." She patted one of the brick walls. "I'll be back. We'll get you fixed up in no time."

Maybe she was going crazy, talking to a building, but if going crazy was what it took to feel a little flame of excitement burning in her chest again, she would take it.

Her apartment was exactly six minutes away from the building. She timed it. She drove east along Lake Street and followed the road as it curved north along the coast of the bay Crooked Bay was named for. The apartment building was on the west side of the road directly across from the bay. There was a small path down to the beach on the other side of the road, which was one of the reasons she had chosen that apartment over the others Clare had gone to look at for her.

Her apartment was the one on the lower right when she faced the building, and the small patio looked out at the bay. She had fallen in love with it as soon as Clare sent her the pictures, and it looked just as promising in person.

She parked next to the moving truck Jace had

rented and got out, waving at Layla as she came out of the apartment building.

"Good, Jace was getting worried about you," Layla said. Her blonde hair was tied back into a ponytail, and it looked like she had been working hard. Theresa would have to ask Jace what sort of gift his girlfriend would like as thanks for all the help. She realized, with a surge of guilt, that she had barely taken the time to get to know the girl.

"I stopped off at the crêperie first," she said. "I wanted to see it again."

"We drove by on our way here. It's really cute. I can't wait to see what you do with it."

The two of them found a heavy box to carry into her apartment together. The building was older, but the apartment had recently been redone. The white carpets on the floors were new, and the walls were painted a soft cream color. It was one bedroom, one bathroom, and the kitchen, dining room, and living room were all one part of the same open area, with a counter dividing the kitchen and the dining room.

It was a lot smaller than her house had been, but she didn't need much space just for her. Besides, she would be spending most of her time at the crêperie.

It was well into the evening by the time they had unloaded everything she had marked for the apartment. There were more boxes in the truck, which they brought to a self-storage facility. She had rented a storage unit there, still not ready to get rid of many of Nicolas's things even though a three-bedroom house held a lot more than a one-bedroom apartment could fit. One day, she would go through everything and figure out what she wanted to donate, what she wanted to keep, and what she wanted to throw away, but she wasn't ready yet.

It was getting dark by the time they finished. Clare, who could be a hard worker when she wanted to, looked beat and said as much. She gave Theresa a tight hug, then glanced at her phone. "I'm going to head home. I've got a palm reading in half an hour, and I want to freshen up first. It's a new client, and I've always got to be on my game with them. Will you be all right? Do you want me to come over afterward?"

"I think I want to settle in on my own tonight," Theresa said. "Maybe we could get lunch tomorrow?"

"Oh, yes. That's a great idea. I'll start introducing you to people around town, too. Everyone's going to be interested in meeting the newest small-business owner."

Theresa smiled and told her it was a plan. It was going to be strange, living so close to her cousin, someone she had babysat as a child and then only seen a couple of times per year as an adult, but she thought it would be nice.

Then it was time to say goodbye to Jace and Layla. Her son gave her a bone-crushing hug, and Layla gave her a much gentler one.

"You sure you're all right here alone, Mom?"

"I'll be fine," she told him. "I'm going to go start unpacking in my apartment. You guys should get going. It's late, and I don't want you to be driving too long in the dark."

"All right. Call me if you need anything?"

"I will," she said. "Thank you both so much for helping."

She waved as they got into the truck and pulled away from the storage facility. Then she made sure her storage unit was locked, got back into her vehicle, and started the engine. It was time to head back to the apartment. It didn't feel like home yet. She didn't know yet if any place could feel like home without her husband, but she was willing to try.

CHAPTER THREE

"There we go," Theresa said, standing back and putting her hands on her hips. She stared at the two pictures she had just hung on the wall behind the counter. The one on the left was the picture of her and Nicolas on their honeymoon in France. The one on the right was a black and white photograph of her grandmother, also in France. The woman had immigrated to the United States in her late twenties, but had always retained a love for her homeland, which she had passed on to her daughter and then, her granddaughter. She was the one who had taught Theresa how to make crêpes, and who had shared with Theresa her love of cooking and the French language and culture, indirectly leading her to meet Nicolas in college. Theresa thought she would be proud to know that she was opening a crêperie. She had passed away a few years ago, and she missed the older woman dearly.

The pictures were the first in a long line of things she wanted to get done today at the crêperie. She knew she would have to come up with a business name soon, but it was harder than she had expected. Coming up with the perfect name that hadn't already been taken? She had spent two months thinking on it and didn't feel any closer than she had when she started.

Hanging the photos was by far the easiest thing she had on her list. Today was all about cleaning and deciding what she needed to buy for this place. She was afraid that list was going to get very long indeed. It was intimidating, but despite how she was jumping into this feetfirst without any real experience, she felt more alive than she had in a long time.

She played some music on her phone, turned the volume up, then paused to make a note that she needed to buy a radio. She had a feeling there would be a lot of quiet times in the crêperie when she would want to listen to music while she worked.

Then she started mopping. She had gone to the general store to get some cleaning supplies and had done research on how to properly clean hardwood floors. She wasn't sure yet whether they would need to be professionally refinished, or if a good cleaning and waxing would make them serviceable. She got to work, mopping and scrubbing and cleaning, dumping the water in the bathroom sink since she didn't want to dirty the kitchen.

By the time she finished the floor in the main room, having avoided waxing herself into a corner at the last minute, it was time to go to lunch with Clare. The freshly waxed floors should be dry by the time she got back, then she could see how they looked.

Clare wanted to meet for lunch at Club King, a delicatessen Theresa had been to a few times before on her visits to Crooked Bay. They had great sandwiches and soup, and she thought she might get something to take home with her for dinner. She hadn't had time to go grocery shopping yet; all she'd done the night before was start unpacking her bedroom, find her pajamas, make her bed, and go to sleep.

Club King was farther west down Lake Street, on the other side of the road, toward the end of the downtown strip. Since the weather was nice, Theresa decided to walk the short distance. Being able to use her own two feet as transportation was a new experience; back home, she'd had to drive whenever she wanted to go somewhere. Now, she could even walk to work if she wanted to leave twenty minutes early. It was a new world. A fresh start. Just what she wanted.

Clare was already at Club King when Theresa arrived. She was seated at a small table by the window, talking to a woman who looked to be about Theresa's age, maybe a few years older. The other woman was standing by the table, leaning against the edge of it with her hip cocked, her graying brown hair pulled back into a tight braid. She glanced up when Theresa came in, and Clare turned around, smiled, and waved her over.

"There you are. I told you I'd start introducing you to people, didn't I? This is Dora Keighley. She owns Club King. Dora, this is my cousin, Theresa Tremblay. She's opening a crêperie in the building that coffee shop used to be in."

"Levi's place?" Dora asked, giving Theresa a measuring look. "You do know what happened there, right?"

"I heard he was murdered," Theresa said. She took the seat across from Clare, setting her purse down on the table. "But the person who did it was caught."

"Sure he was," Dora said. She sounded skeptical, but didn't elaborate. "Well, as long as you know what you're getting into. Levi's murder shook the whole town. People might take some time to warm up to the idea of a new business there so soon. I wish you the best, though; I haven't had a good crêpe in years. When are you opening?"

"It's going to be a while," Theresa said. "I've got a lot of work to do to prepare the building. Once I have a solid date, I'll start advertising around town."

"You're welcome to hang a flyer in here if you'd like to," Dora said. She shook Theresa's hand briskly. "It's nice to meet you. I'll let you look over the menu for a few minutes, then I'll come back and get your order. You came just in time for the lunch rush, so we're going to be busy. If you need something, just shout."

Dora hurried away, stopping to check on another table on her way back to the kitchen. Theresa turned to Clare, but before she could greet her cousin, Clare started waving at someone outside the window madly. Theresa turned to see a mailman standing on the other side of the glass. He waved back at her cousin and came around to the deli's door. Clare gestured him over to their table.

"This is another important face to know, Theresa," she said. "This man is Martin Braddock. He delivers most of the mail in town. You'll probably be seeing him a lot."

"She's the one you were telling me about?" Martin asked, giving Theresa another appraising look. She was beginning to wonder what her cousin had been telling these people about her.

Martin was on the older side of middle aged, gray and balding. He had deep wrinkles and tanned skin which spoke of a long career spent outdoors, but despite that, or maybe because of it, he looked spry and healthy.

"I'd like to be one of the first to welcome you to Crooked Bay, ma'am," he said. "Like Clare said, I'll be the one delivering all of your mail, at least for your business. I'm not sure if I'll be taking care of your residential mail. Where did you end up renting?"

"Bayside," Clare said before Theresa could answer. "Those little apartments just north of town."

"Ah, that won't be me then. You'll have Betsy Greene for your residential mail. She's a good woman. If you run into any problems, either of us will be happy to help you."

"Thanks," Theresa said. "It was nice to meet you."

He nodded and made a motion as if he was tipping an invisible hat at her, gave a small wave goodbye to Clare, then stopped by the front counter to drop off the deli's mail. Theresa turned back to her cousin, raising her eyebrows.

"Do you know everyone in town?"

Clare laughed. "Not quite everyone, but I make a point of saying hi to people when I can. It's good for business. Plus, these are good folks."

Despite having asked her multiple times over the years, Theresa still wasn't exactly sure what it was Clare did for a living. She knew palm readings and other fortuneteller-type stuff was involved, and she thought at one point Clare had mentioned being a life coach, and there had been a phase where she'd painted pictures of people's pets, but it all seemed very eclectic. She supposed being a known and well-liked face around town would help to get her clients regardless of what her business actually was.

"I'm looking forward to getting to know them," Theresa said, honestly. She might spend the rest of her life in this town. She wanted to make friends.

Theresa ordered the deli's namesake club sandwich and got a container of beef and barley stew to go. She and Clare spent the next half hour talking about Theresa's plans for the crêperie. She was feeling a little overwhelmed, and while Clare did have a tendency to run off on wild goose chases, she was a smart woman who gave good advice and tended to think outside the box. That was ingenious for working around some of Theresa's problems, like figuring out a menu.

"I think you're trying to do too much," Clare said when Theresa showed her the list of things she wanted to serve. "First of all, you're opening a crêperie. You can cut out all this other stuff—" She gestured at the list of desserts and other food ideas Theresa had written down, "For now. You don't need all these drinks either. Sure, people like smoothies, but they aren't going to your crêperie for a smoothie. You can get away with just serving some good coffee and having a fridge full of other drinks. Just focus on your crêpes. And speaking of focusing, I don't think you need a million different crêpes to start out with. Just have, like, three sweet ones and three savory ones. Get those down pat, figure out what people like, and experiment with different ones from there. I can guarantee you the people in Crooked Bay aren't expecting a huge, multipage menu. You're probably going to find that most people order the same one or two things anyway."

"You're right," Theresa said, taking her phone back. "I'm just so excited. I want everything to go perfectly."

"Terra, dear cousin, I have horrible news for you," Clare said, taking her hand and squeezing it as she gazed into her eyes. "There isn't the tiniest chance in the world that this is going to go perfectly. You've lost that battle before you even started. The sooner you come to terms with that, the happier you'll be."

Theresa rolled her eyes and pulled her hand away, but she knew her cousin had a point. What she was envisioning in her head—a smooth grand opening and a packed restaurant every day after, with every review five stars—was a fantasy. She was going to make mistakes, and probably a lot of them. She had to be prepared for that.

She finished her sandwich—which was probably one of the best club sandwiches she had ever had—and got a bag for her container of soup before they left the deli. Clare checked the time on her phone. "I've got to meet a client in about an hour and a half, but I've got a little bit of time to kill if you want to get coffee before I head out."

"At Ridiculous Beans?" Theresa asked. "I haven't been there for years. Nicolas used to love that place, because of the name."

"Well, it's the only coffee shop in town now, so, yeah. It's just down the block from here."

"Let's go," Theresa said. She knew getting coffee

there would give her a wave of nostalgia, but she thought she might be ready to start trying to find reasons to smile at these old memories instead of avoiding them whenever possible. Besides, the reminder of the fact that her little building had been a coffee shop not too long ago served as a good distraction from memories of her late husband.

Had buying a building with such a sordid history been a mistake? She hoped not. There was no going back now, and besides, she liked the little brick building with its crooked door and old floors. It had character.

Ridiculous Beans wasn't as busy as the deli had been. There was only one person in line in front of them. She and Clare waited until it was their turn, then stepped up to the counter. Instead of ordering, Clare said, "Is your boss in? Alyson? I've got someone I want to introduce her to."

The young woman blinked. "Um, yeah, I think she is. Do you want me to go get her?"

"I'd love that, thanks," Clare said. The woman ducked into the back, and Clare turned to Theresa. "Alyson is great, she's been a client for years. If you've got questions about coffee, she could point you towards some good machines."

"Does she do palm readings with you?" Theresa

asked, trying to figure out just what her cousin was known for.

"Sorry, I keep all that stuff confidential. My clients take it all very seriously, and I try to respect that."

Theresa wondered if Clare took her palm readings and psychic business seriously. Despite all of the trouble she got into when she was younger, and her occasional poorly thought-out ideas, Clare had never seemed very superstitious or into new age beliefs, at least not until she started whatever her current career path was. She wanted to ask, but now wasn't the time. The employee came back with a woman who looked to be around Clare's age. Alyson beamed as soon as she saw Clare.

"It's been a while since you stopped in." She came around the counter to give Clare a quick hug. "What brings you here today?"

"I wanted to introduce you to my cousin, Theresa," Clare said, turning to her. "She bought that building that used to be Levi's coffee shop. She's going to turn it into a crêperie."

Alyson looked at Theresa with an odd expression on her face. It only lasted for a moment, but it reminded Theresa of the other considering looks the people her cousin had introduced her to had given her.

Were they expecting someone like Clare only to be disappointed by her own more subdued presence? Were they wondering why in the world she had bought the murder building? Or had Clare told them about Nicolas's futile battle with pancreatic cancer? Were these looks of pity? She couldn't help wondering what they knew about her. She'd wanted anonymity when she relocated, and hoped Clare hadn't spread around too much information about her.

"It's nice to meet you," Alyson said. She gave Theresa's hand a perfunctory shake, then retreated back around the counter. "What can I get the two of you? It's on the house today."

Theresa ordered an iced vanilla latte while Clare got a chai tea. As they waited for their drinks to be made, she couldn't help but wonder just what her cousin had gotten her into. She hadn't done much research on the murder that happened in her building, and now she was beginning to think that had been a mistake.

CHAPTER FOUR

Theresa found her laptop and charging cord when she got home that evening and settled down on her couch to try to find some answers to her questions. She didn't have Wi-Fi yet—the installers were supposed to come tomorrow—so she had to use her phone's hotspot to access the internet. She didn't know the full name of the man who had been killed, so she typed, *Levi, murder, coffee shop, Crooked Bay* into the search bar. Thankfully, it came up with a handful of articles on the first try.

Owner of Local Coffee Shop, Levi Elwyn, Victim of Suspected Homicide

She clicked the article.

Police were called to a business on Lake Street in downtown Crooked Bay today, where an employee discovered his boss's body when he arrived to open the coffee shop. The cause of death is currently unknown. More information will be forthcoming. If you know anything about this incident, please contact the number below.

Underneath that, there was an updated section, dated a few months later.

Employee Found Guilty in Murder of Boss

Ben Hughes, 21, was found guilty in the murder of his boss, Levi Elwyn, 53. Stabbed twice from behind, Levi died of blood loss after his assailant fled, only for Ben to return later that morning to pretend he found his boss's body when he arrived to open the coffee shop. We ask for your respect toward the family of the deceased in this trying time. Ben's sentencing will take place next Monday at 12 p.m..

All the other articles she found said pretty much the same things. They were all dated a few months ago at the newest. Further down the search page, she found a link to where the article had been posted to a social media site where people had commented below it.

No way did Ben kill him!

Ben's a good guy. He didn't do this.

I don't believe it for a second. They have the wrong man.

Why on earth would Ben kill his boss? I was one of his best friends. He was leaving for college in a few weeks. He never complained about his boss once, he enjoyed his job at the coffee shop, and he said he was going to be leaving it. The evidence was planted. Free Ben.

Evidence? Theresa read through the article again, but she didn't see any mention of evidence. There was frustratingly little on the case overall, and Theresa closed her computer with a sharp snap. None of the commenters seemed to think Ben had been involved with the murder, and Dora, the deli's owner, had seemed skeptical that the killer had been caught too. Was Clare wrong? Was Levi's killer still out there?

It was bad enough that the crêperie was the scene of a murder, but what if the killer came back when she finally had her grand opening?

Fighting back a surge of unease, Theresa rose to her feet to make sure the patio door and the apartment's front door were both locked. Crooked Bay was supposed to be a safe town, but she wasn't sure how true that was anymore.

She spent the first part of the next day at her apartment, unpacking and waiting on the internet installation. The installation crew didn't get there until noon, but thankfully the install itself was easy; most of the equipment was already there, and they just had to give her a router and get her service started. By the time she left her apartment, it was looking more like a home, though it still didn't feel like *her* home.

She drove into town and parked in the shared lot behind the crêperie. She was getting hungry, but she wanted to get a little cleaning done before she went out for lunch. When she did finally take her break, she wanted to do some shopping.

She unlocked the back door to the building and stepped inside. The entrance led directly into the kitchen, and she looked up at the high ceilings, smiling. Her apartment might not feel like home yet, but this place sure did.

She grabbed her cleaning supplies, which she had left in the storeroom, and went into the main room to get to work. She had just sprayed a few squirts of the cleaning solution onto the counter when she heard someone knock on the front door. Through the window set into it, she saw Martin Braddock waving at her. The mailman didn't look as friendly and good natured as he had yesterday. Instead, he looked upset, almost frantic as he gestured for her to come out of the building.

Setting the cleaning spray aside, she walked over to the front door, unlocked it, and said, "How can I help you?"

"Have you seen it?" he asked.

She frowned. "Seen what?"

His gaze drifted upward. She stepped out of the building and onto the sidewalk beside him and looked where his eyes had been drawn. What she saw made her heart sink like a stone. Scrawled above the door in big white, spray-painted letters were the words, *Go Away!*

Her breath caught. A mixture of anger and hurt roiled inside her. What had she done to deserve this? How had she possibly gotten off on such a wrong foot with someone already? And how would she ever get that paint off of the bricks? She took a deep, shaky breath and reached for her phone. She didn't know if there was anything the police could do about this, but it couldn't hurt to ask.

CHAPTER FIVE

Martin couldn't wait for the police to arrive; he had to keep walking his mail route, but he told her he would check in with her when he passed by on his way back through town. He seemed sympathetic, which helped a little bit, but Theresa was still upset. She knew this was probably the doing of just one person, but it hurt to think the town didn't want her.

When the police did show up, it wasn't in the shiny new SUV she was used to seeing back home. It was an old-fashioned police car, which looked at least as old as Jace was. The officer who stepped out of it looked about the same age as her son as well.

"Hello, ma'am. I'm Officer Fenwick. You had an issue with graffiti?"

She turned to gesture at the writing on the

building behind her. "I found this when I got to work today. Can you, I don't know, ask around to figure out who did it? If it was just some kids, I don't care about pressing charges as long as they don't do it again, but…" She trailed off, unable to express how unsettled reading about Levi's murder had made her feel.

Officer Fenwick frowned as he gazed up at the graffiti. "I can ask around, but I doubt anyone will fess up. What I *can* do is take a report down, and if it happens again or they graffiti somewhere else and we catch the person, it will give added weight to any charges pressed against them. I've got to say, though, this isn't the first time we've had trouble with this building."

"Are you talking about the murder?"

He shook his head. "Well, there was that too, but we caught the guy behind that. It was a few months before then, when old Levi started having issues with people leaving graffiti on the windows and slipping nasty letters into the mailbox. We never caught the person responsible, but we sent out a PSA reminding people that interfering with a mailbox is a federal crime, and that stopped that. My guess is it's the same people who were harassing him."

"Do you think it's just because I'm new? An easy target?"

He shrugged. "Could be. I'll suggest to you the same thing I suggested to him; invest in some good security cameras. Put them up somewhere obvious. That should be enough to scare whoever's doing this away."

"Thanks," she said, mentally adding yet another item to her shopping list. "I'll do that. There's nothing you can do now, though?"

"Like I said, I'll take a report." He eyed her, as if he was really taking her in for the first time. "You're opening a new business here, right? What was it, pancakes?"

"Crêpes," she said. "Sort of like French pancakes."

"I know what crêpes are," he said, sounding amused. "I'm looking forward to eating here once you're open. We don't have enough restaurants in this town. I'll keep an eye out for you, maybe drive by a bit more often than I usually do. You just let me know if you have any more trouble, okay?"

"I will," she said. "Thank you."

He leaned against his car as he wrote his report and took some photos of the graffiti. She watched him from inside as she scrubbed the counter, and just as he finished up, she realized she had one last question for him. She opened the front door, stuck her head out, and said, "Wait, Officer Fenwick?"

"What do you need?" he asked, not sounding unfriendly, just a bit bored.

"Do you have any idea how I can clean that paint off?"

"I think Levi had some luck with paint thinner and rubbing alcohol. You should be able to get both at the hardware store."

Even though the young police officer hadn't actually done much, his visit had made her feel better. She finished cleaning the counter, then decided to take a break and go to the hardware store to buy a ladder and cleaning supplies for the graffiti. She would see if they had any security cameras too, otherwise she would have to make a trip into a bigger town or order some online. She didn't want this to happen again.

She put the cleaning supplies away and was getting her list ready to go when someone else knocked on the door. This time when she looked out the window, she saw Clare waving at her. She waved back and walked over to unlock the door.

"I was just about to head out," she said. "I've got to go to the hardware store."

"Did you see what someone did to your building?" Clare asked, pointing up.

"Unfortunately, I did. I've already had the police out."

"Do they know who did it?"

"No, but it sounds like the previous tenant had some issues with something similar."

"I can't believe someone would do this after everything that happened with Levi," Clare said, glaring up at the graffiti as if her gaze could burn it away. "You'd think the fact that someone was murdered here would keep the kids away."

Theresa hesitated, then pulled the door open further. "Can you come in, Clare? I want to talk to you about something."

Her cousin raised an eyebrow but did as she was asked. Theresa shut the door behind her, then put her hands on her hips. "I've been doing more research into that murder, and it sounds like a lot of towns-people aren't convinced that Ben guy had anything to do with it. It's my fault for not doing more research before I bought the place, but you sounded pretty certain they'd caught the right guy, Clare. Is there any chance that the police were wrong, and the killer is still out there?"

"Why are you asking me?" Clare asked. "I didn't know either of them that well. I was just going by what I read in the paper and what I heard people saying around town. The police found the knife Levi was stabbed with in the back of Ben's car. It seems pretty open and shut to me."

Clare had a point. Theresa wondered if she was just being paranoid. Coming to work to find the graffiti right after she'd spent an evening reading about the murder must have set her on edge.

"If I get killed because I bought this place on your advice, I'm definitely coming back to haunt you."

"Psychic, remember?" Clare asked, wiggling her fingers at her. "I'll just Google how to do a séance or something. I bet I could charge for it, too, especially if it was a real haunting." She tapped her fingers on her chin, considering, then grinned. "Come on, let's go get the supplies, and I'll help you clean that spray paint up. Don't let this get you down, Theresa. Whoever did this is just one person. The town's happy to have you here, and so am I."

CHAPTER SIX

Before Theresa knew it, she had been in Crooked Bay for a week. A week of unpacking, a week of cleaning and scrubbing every inch of the crêperie. A week spent hoping and praying she hadn't made the wrong choice by moving here.

Thankfully, she hadn't had any more problems since the graffiti. The police hadn't found the person or people responsible for it yet, but as long as it didn't happen again, she was willing to let bygones be bygones. The paint thinner had managed to take the spray paint off the bricks, and while the chemical had left noticeably lighter streaks on the brick, it wasn't very easy to spot unless she was looking for it.

The weekend arrived, and her son was arriving with it. Theresa knew she couldn't expect Jace to visit her every week, not when she lived three hours away and he had a busy life of his own, but she was glad he was coming out this weekend. She knew he was checking up on her and wished he wouldn't see her as someone he had to take care of. She hoped it would make him feel better to see that she was settling in.

She woke up early to put the finishing touches on her apartment. The night before had marked her last night of unpacking, and this morning she collapsed the boxes and stored them in the front closet, then vacuumed, made sure her bed was neatly made, and the throw blanket was folded and laid over the back of the couch. She lit a candle to help make the apartment smell less like the cleaning sprays she had used on everything, and pulled the sliding glass balcony door part of the way open to let fresh air come in through the screen. There was a breeze from the lake. It was a little bit chilly, and it had been raining on and off all morning, but she liked the crisp smell of the air.

By the time Jace pulled into the apartment's small parking lot, Theresa's apartment not only looked put together, but was beginning to feel just as cozy and comfortable as she had hoped. It had been a busy week, juggling setting her new home up and getting the crêperie ready for its first delivery of furniture and appliances. Jace's visit had given her the final push she needed to put the finishing touches on it; now, she thought, her apartment would actually be a place of relaxation instead of an added stressor to her already busy days.

She greeted her son with a warm hug and then gave him the grand tour. He had seen her apartment when it was empty, and then filled with boxes straight off of the moving truck. She hoped that seeing it like this, with all of her things from home, would assure him that she was comfortable here.

"This is lovely, Mom," he said when they had circled through the small apartment and returned to the living room. He sat down on the couch, kicked his feet up onto the coffee table, and looked out the glass patio door. "This is an amazing view. I bet you spend a lot of time here, just looking at the lake."

She sat next to him and followed his gaze. The patio looked out to the road, but past that were the long beach grasses and a sandy slope down to the shore. It was a breezy day, and she could see white waves rushing in from the bay.

"I love the view," she replied, truthfully. "I haven't had much time to just relax yet, but now that this place is unpacked, I should have a chance to enjoy it more."

"I hope you haven't been too busy."

"I'd like to see you 'not be too busy' in the week following a move," she said, laughing. She rose to her feet. "Come on, let's go to the crêperie. The furniture should arrive Monday or Tuesday. You'll probably never see it empty like this again. It looks a lot better with everything cleaned and polished and repainted."

"Did you think of a name yet?" he asked as he followed her over to the door and sat on the bench she'd had since before he was born to tie his shoes.

"Not yet," she said. "I know, I know. I've got to settle on something. Maybe you can help me brainstorm while you're here."

They took her crossover into town. On their way, they passed the beachside park that was on the shore just where Lake Street curved north. It wasn't particularly busy so early in the year, but there were a few people hitting a volleyball back and forth. She and Jace stopped there to walk down to the beach and enjoy the fresh air. They left when it started raining. On their way back to the car, he asked if they could stop and get some coffee.

"Sure," she said. "If she's in, I can introduce you to Alyson. I think she and I are becoming friends."

Despite how busy she had been, she had made an effort to be outgoing and social with the people Clare introduced her to. She chatted with Martin the mailman when she saw him going by, had stopped by the deli for lunch a few times and asked how Dora was doing when she saw her there, and had spent one long dinner at the local diner with Alyson and Clare, chatting about every topic under the sun. She hadn't been so social since Nicolas died. It was exhausting, but she was surprised to find how much she enjoyed it.

As she suspected, Jace was pleased that she was making friends. She drove them past the crêperie and looped around the block so she could park on the opposite side of the road, in front of Ridiculous Beans.

"I remember this place," her son said. He was grinning as he undid his seatbelt. "Dad loved the name. I think he bought a new coffee mug from them every year we visited."

She smiled. "I'm glad you remember that. Tell you what, I'll get you a mug while we're here. And one to bring home to Layla, if you think she'd like one. How is she doing, by the way?"

"She's doing well. I actually have something I wanted to talk to you about—but let's get our coffee first."

She raised an eyebrow as she followed him into

the coffee shop. She was curious, but her son could be just as stubborn as Nicolas was, so she knew pushing him wouldn't do anything but make him irritated. For the first time since he'd asked if she was free today, she wondered if this visit had to do with something other than just checking up on her.

They hurried into the warm, coffee-scented building, leaving the chilly rain behind. It was a shame the weather wasn't nicer today, but there was something cozy about this weather when she was somewhere dry and cozy. Maybe she'd curl up on the couch after Jace left and read a book while she watched the rain pelt the waters of the bay.

A few of the tables in the coffee shop were occupied, but there was no one in line, so they made their way directly to the counter. Alyson was occupied at the far end of the room, and there was no barista in sight.

"Hey, Carrie, can you get me the dish tub from the kitchen? I think it might work better." Alyson looked up at Theresa and Jace, then looked around the room and sighed. Straightening up, she wiped her brow and came toward them. "Sorry about that, I thought Carrie was still up here. She must have stepped into the other room. Just give me a sec, and I'll take your order."

Theresa was finally able to see what Alyson had

been working on and realized she had been trying to line up a plastic bucket to catch drips from the ceiling. The coffee shop's roof was leaking.

"There's no hurry," Theresa assured her as the other woman washed her hands. "Is everything all right here?"

"Other than the building being one good storm away from turning into a pile of rubble, it's all just peachy." Alyson dried her hands, then turned to them with a grimace. "Sorry, you came in for some caffeine, not to listen to me complain."

"I don't mind," Theresa said. "It's good to know what problems I might end up facing at the crêperie. Is it expensive to fix a leak like that?"

"It's not the money," Alyson said, wrinkling her nose. "It's the landlord. He's refusing to hire someone to actually fix the problem. Last year, he went up there and laid down a tarp, but it must have blown away or gotten a hole in it. I wish I could relocate, but the same guy owns half the commercial buildings in town, and when places do go up for sale, they're snatched up in seconds, it seems like."

"Oh." Had Alyson wanted to buy the building that would soon become the crêperie? "I hope you find a good solution."

"I'm half tempted to just knock a bigger hole in

the roof and force him to do something besides half measures." She shook her head, then forced a smile. "Anyway, how can I help you today?"

"We're here to get some warm drinks. I'd also like to introduce my son, Jace. He's visiting for the day."

"It's nice to meet you," Alyson said. "I'm good friends with your ... aunt, is it? Clare has been reading tarot cards for me for years. I know a lot of people think it's a load of hocus pocus, but she's been really spot on with a lot."

"She's my cousin." He glanced at Theresa. "Or, well, second cousin? Or cousin once removed? I can never remember how all that works, but she's my mom's cousin. I remember she tried to teach me to read tarot once, but that was during my trading card phase, and I wasn't very interested since none of my friends had them."

"You should give it another chance," Alyson said. "Maybe it runs in the family. So, what can I get the two of you today?"

They ordered their drinks, and once she had made them, Alyson returned to trying to catch the various leaks from the roof. Theresa wished her luck, and she and Jace returned to the car. She looped around the block at the main intersection so she could park on the correct side of the road in front of the crêperie.

She wanted to give Jace the full experience of walking in through the front door, just like her customers would get.

"Mom, this is amazing," he said as he entered the building. "This is perfect for your crêperie."

She smiled, glad at the praise. She agreed with him; she couldn't have asked for a better building. Now that the floor had been cleaned and polished, the bricks scrubbed, the counter touched up with fresh shellac, and the windows cleaned to a sparkle, it looked warm and welcoming. The pictures of her and Nicolas and of her grandmother were still the only items hanging on the walls, but she had an order of French decor on the way.

"Just wait until the next time you come. You won't recognize it."

"I'm so happy for you," he said, pulling her into a hug, though he was careful not to jostle their coffee.

"Thank you, Jace. I'm happy too. I think this was a good change, and I'm glad you helped push me into it." She smiled and patted his cheek. "Come on, let's sit down and you can talk to me about whatever it was you wanted to talk to me about. Don't think I forgot."

"Right."

She didn't miss how he suddenly seemed nervous as she led him over to the folding table and chairs she had set up in the back part of her main room so she had somewhere to sit while she ate her lunches and wrote her lists.

His hands must have been shaking, because as he set his coffee down on the table, some splashed out through the mouthpiece of the cup's lid. "Shoot, I'm sorry."

"Don't worry, I've got paper towels in the kitchen. I'll be right back."

She strode through the door behind the front counter, shooting one last, concerned look back at her son. Whatever he wanted to tell her must be serious. For the life of her, she couldn't imagine what it would be.

She was so distracted, she didn't notice something was wrong until she heard a crunch under her shoe. When she looked down at the floor, she froze. Broken glass littered the kitchen tiles. She tilted her head up to see that two of the high windows had been shattered.

There were two fist-sized rocks lying amongst the broken glass on the floor. She didn't see a note, but the message was clear. The graffiti had been just the beginning.

"Mom?" Jace's voice came in through the kitchen door. "Did you find a paper towel?"

"Coming, sweetie." She snatched up the roll of paper towels and hurried out of the kitchen before her son could come looking for her. She hadn't told him about the graffiti, and she didn't intend to tell him about this either, at least not yet.

She handed him the roll and then sat down across from him. He cleaned up the mess, then took a deep breath, staring at the crumpled paper towel in his hands.

"Mom ... I asked Layla to marry me."

Theresa's breath caught. "What did she say?"

"She said yes."

"Oh, Jace. I'm so happy for you."

She moved around the table to hug him, blinking against the prickling in her eyes. They were young— only twenty-two—but she hadn't been any older when she and Nicolas got married. She wished she had made the effort to get to know Layla better, and she desperately hoped that Jace had made the right decision, but above all of that, she was happy for her son.

Everything was changing. Only time would tell if those changes were all for the better.

CHAPTER SEVEN

"Seriously? They can't do anything?"

Jace had gone home two hours ago, and Theresa had called Clare to help her patch the windows. She wouldn't be able to schedule a repair until Monday, and she didn't want the rain to wreck anything before then.

"Officer Fenwick said he'll keep an eye out for me and ask around to see if anyone in the area saw or heard anything, but what else *could* he do?" Theresa asked. Her neck was craned as she looked up at her cousin; Clare was high up on the ladder, duct taping a cut up piece of tarp over one of the broken windows while Theresa steadied the base. Neither of them were exactly pro handymen, but she figured the tarps should at least keep out the moisture. Unless the wind ended up blowing them away, anyway.

"I don't know, dust those rocks for prints? Post a squad car in the parking lot overnight?" Clare ripped the tape and smoothed it over the edge of the tarp, then looked down. "You're trying to start a business here. You haven't done anything wrong. It isn't fair."

"Doesn't Crooked Bay only have, like, three squad cars? I don't blame him for not offering to post someone here overnight; I can't imagine they have more than one person on night shift anyway. No one's getting hurt; I don't want to take time away from the police keeping people safe."

"Theresa, dear, the only criminals the local police ever have to deal with are people who go fifteen over on the road along the shore. We aren't exactly a hotbed of crime." She slapped another strip of tape across the edge of the tarp. "Well, not usually. Shoot, I'm out of tape."

Clare let the empty cardboard ring fall, and Theresa ducked out of the way, letting it land on the wet concrete beside her while her cousin fished another roll out of the large pouch pocket of the sweatshirt she was wearing. Theresa had offered to be the one to go up the ladder, but Clare had pointed out that her luck this past week had already been pretty lackluster. Climbing up to the top of a tall ladder was just asking for something bad to happen. Theresa didn't quite agree with her cousin's logic, but she hadn't put up much of a fight. She wasn't a fan of heights.

"I ordered security cameras—they'll be here next week. I doubt I'll have any more issues after that. For all we know, this is just the work of some teenagers with nothing better to do who think the building is still empty. They might stop once it's obvious a business is occupying it again."

"If you find out it is some kids being dumb, let me know who it is. I'll offer a free tarot reading to their parents and put some good old supernatural fear in them. Maybe that will get them to keep a better eye on their children. There's no excuse for this sort of property destruction."

"Do you really believe in all that stuff?" Theresa asked. Clare looked down at her and almost fumbled the fresh roll of tape. She lunged to catch it, and the ladder jolted. Theresa looked up at her cousin with wide eyes, her grip tight on the aluminum frame, but the other woman didn't seem shaken in the slightest. She made a humming noise as she considered the question.

"In a strict sense, no. I don't think there's some

magical force that speaks through the cards, or that people have a destiny that is written on their palms. But I think it can make people consider problems from angles they wouldn't otherwise. There's something to the idea that it opens a window to your subconscious. A lot of people play up the mumbo-jumbo, but really it's just a way to sit down and consider something with less bias. The house-reading thing I do works the same way. A lot of the couples who hire me are young and excited—it's their first house. They tend to overlook issues like cracks in the foundation and mysterious water stains or sketchy neighbors because they're so in love with the idea of being homeowners. I'm there to draw extra attention to those things, so they don't get so lost in their dream that they ignore what's right in front of their face. Most of what I do these days is basically therapy with a side of home inspection, I just couch it in mystical terms since I don't need a license for that."

"I can't decide if that makes you more or less of a scam artist," Theresa said. "What happened to that psychic painting thing you were doing?"

"Eh, I got bored of that. Way too much sitting in one spot, not enough running around and chatting with people. Anyway, I think I'm done up here. You got the ladder?"

"I won't let it slip."

Clare made her way down safely. Once she was at the bottom, they both looked up at the windows. The blue tarp was ugly, but at least the duct tape seemed to be working to keep it up there, for now. She hoped it wouldn't take too long to get the windows repaired.

"I don't think this is just kids being kids," her cousin said at last. "It's not like Crooked Bay has had a rash of similar problems, and didn't Officer Fenwick tell you the previous owner had problems too? This seems centered on the building for some reason. I'll try to poke around and see if I can get in contact with whoever sold it to Levi. Maybe they went through something similar; maybe there's a neighbor who doesn't like having another business next door or something."

"Thanks," Theresa said. "I hate that this is an issue at all. Who doesn't like crêpes?"

"People on a low carb diet?"

"I saw a recipe for low carb crêpes just the other day. I need to try it out soon."

"If you ever need a taste tester, I'm your gal," Clare said. She helped Theresa collapse the ladder and store it in the building, then glanced at her phone. "I've got to head out. Are you going home soon, or are you going to stick around and try to catch the window-breaking graffiti artists in the act?"

"I might stick around for a bit. Not to play at being a private eye, but to make sure everything is ready for the furniture delivery Monday. Speaking of taste testing, though, do you want to come over for dinner sometime soon? Maybe Monday? I still need to finish grocery shopping."

"Be safe."

They embraced quickly, then Clare went to her car, and Theresa went in through the crêperie's back door. She really needed to finalize a name for the place; it would take a couple weeks for a custom sign to get made and delivered, and she wanted to open as soon as possible.

After doing one last walkthrough, she sat at her little folding table and opened her notepad. She had roughly sketched where she wanted the tables and chairs, to make it easier on the movers, and tried to imagine what it would look like when it was all done, with the smell of crêpes in the air and her tables filled with customers.

She heard the sound of her mailbox closing. It was a metal box on the wall just outside the building's front door, and she'd gotten used to the sound of

Martin dropping mail in it every day, so it was a second before she realized something was off.

It was dark out. The mail came early, around noon. It was far too late for Martin to be doing his rounds. She glanced up and thought she saw a dark form peering in the window for a second before they moved away.

Without pausing to think about it, she rose to her feet and strode over to the door. Unlocking it, she stepped onto the sidewalk, but whoever was out there must have ducked into the alley or gone into another building.

She looked both ways down the sidewalk, then opened her mailbox. There was a catalogue full of ads from this morning's mail, and a blank, sealed envelope without a stamp or return address sitting on top of it.

She took both pieces of mail from the box and went back inside, locking the door behind her.

At the table, she set the advertisement aside and opened the envelope, too full of dread to even consider waiting and going to the police with it first. She had to know what it said.

It turned out, knowing didn't help.

Get away while you still can. Next time it won't be

your windows that take damage, it will be you. I always follow through on my threats. Just ask Levi.

That was it. Four sentences, no signature, and blocky writing that looked as if someone had intentionally tried to disguise their handwriting.

It was enough to convince Theresa that Clare had been very, very wrong when she said the person who killed the previous tenant of the building had been caught.

CHAPTER EIGHT

Even with the note, there wasn't much the police
could do. They took it into evidence and promised
they would do their best, but there was no magic
wand. They couldn't pull a suspect out of thin air, and
there was no one in her life Theresa could point them
to. No one had been rude or threatening to her face—
in fact, everyone she had met in Crooked Bay had
gone out of their way to be nice and pleasant to her.
Was one of the smiling faces she had spent the last
week getting to know the killer?

She spent Sunday at her apartment, feeling unsafe
at the thought of being in the empty crêperie alone.
Not telling Jace what was going on filled her with
guilt—she knew he would want to know—but he had
just gotten engaged. She didn't want to take away

from this special time in his life and force him to worry about his mom.

She half expected to get a call from the police that another window had been broken or the entire building had burned down, but Sunday came and went without any further disaster. Before the note, she might have been relieved. Now, she just felt on edge. She didn't know when the person behind the vandalism and the threatening letter would try something else. If they made good on their threat, then she would be the next target.

As she got ready to go into town for the furniture delivery on Monday morning, she wondered seriously if she should throw in the towel. This was a huge change for her, and she had been prepared to have moments of doubt and fear, but she had *not* been prepared for threats and a murder mystery. Pressing forward when the going got tough was one thing. Pressing forward when someone was threatening to hurt her was on an entirely different level.

Maybe she could get her old job back, or if not, find a similar one. She could sublet her apartment, rent a little house back in her old city, and spend her days doing the same thing until she hit retirement age and fell into a different rut.

The thought made her stomach clench. Despite

the vandalism and the threat, she'd felt more alive since she made her decision to take a leap of faith and open a crêperie than she had since Nicolas died. She didn't want to go back to her old life, to basically being a zombie with every day just as miserable as the last.

She was only forty-five. She wanted to *live*.

Of course, getting killed by a violent maniac would cut this new chance at life very short.

Grumbling and torn between the decision to press forward despite the risks or give up, she set off for the crêperie. No matter what she ended up deciding, the furniture delivery was coming in half an hour, and she needed to be there to unlock the door.

Other than one of the tarps covering the broken windows having come partially undone, the crêperie was just how she had left it Saturday evening. It was a relief, or at least, a partial relief. The threat she received had said the person behind the vandalism would come after her next. Maybe the fact that nothing else had happened to the crêperie meant they were going to make good on that threat. As much as she loved the little building, she would much rather it be the target of violence than her own person.

The furniture delivery van pulled up in front of the curb shortly after she arrived. She propped the front door open and walked outside to talk to the two movers, and soon they started unloading the tables, chairs, and various other bits of furniture such as a desk for the office. It was an exciting day, but the excitement was tinged with anxiety. Every time someone walked by or slowed their car to drive around the moving van, she wondered if they were the person responsible for all of the issues she had been having. Paranoia was a new experience for her, and she didn't like it. She tried to imagine what Nicolas would say if he was here. He had never been quick to anger or become upset, but she knew he would have stopped at nothing to protect his loved ones. Would he have insisted that they give up on the building and try to start over elsewhere? Would he have hired a private investigator or an overnight security guard for the crêperie?

She didn't know, and she hated that she didn't know.

"Excuse me."

She had been so lost in thought that she hadn't heard someone approaching her. She jolted and turned to come face-to-face with a man about her own age, maybe a few years older. He had brown hair that was starting to turn gray, and a short beard that was a shade lighter. He was wearing rectangular glasses and a houndstooth jacket that made him look older than he probably was.

"How can I help you?" She turned to face him more fully, and in the process took a step back, wary of anyone who she hadn't known for years at this point.

"Are you Theresa Tremblay?"

She hesitated. "Yes?"

He frowned, probably confused about how uncertain she sounded. "This might sound odd, and I don't usually believe in this kind of thing, but a psychic told me to come find you. She was very insistent."

Despite her wariness, Theresa's lips twitched. "If you don't believe in psychics, why were you seeing one?"

"She came to see me. I'm Liam Shaw." He held out his hand, and she took it out of reflex, shaking it. "I own the used bookstore on the other side of town. The psychic is one of my regulars, and yesterday she came up to me and told me her tarot cards told her to tell me to go find a woman named Theresa Tremblay and answer all her questions. I close the store for lunch anyway, so I figured I might as well at least see what I can help you with."

"Unless this town has a lot of New Age enthusiasts I'm not aware of, I'm guessing the woman you ran into is my cousin, Clare Bardot. I really don't know why she would tell you to come find me." Theresa frowned. "Unless... Do you happen to know who used to own this building before the previous tenant had it?" She gestured at the crêperie.

"That would be my parents," he said. "They sold it about eight years ago. I'm guessing you have questions about it?" He looked unsure, and still a little bit uncertain about the whole thing. Theresa mentally berated Clare; couldn't she have just told the guy what Theresa wanted to know from the get go? She knew her cousin liked playing up her psychic persona, but it was rather irritating in this circumstance.

"It's a long story, but I've been having issues with harassment here for the past week, since I started work on the building. One of the police officers I spoke to indicated the previous tenant had similar issues, and I was wondering if the person who had the building before him experienced the same thing. The police aren't able to do much, and I have no idea who's behind it. It's getting frustrating. They broke two of my windows over the weekend." She hesitated, then added, "And they left me a threatening letter. I gave the note to the police, but I took a picture of it, if you'd like to see. Do you know if your parents had any similar issues?"

He looked serious now, no longer prepared to laugh this whole meeting off as some awkward joke. "As a matter of fact, they did. There wasn't any vandalism, but they got a few strange letters when they sold the building. I don't have them on hand, but I think my mother has them somewhere. She lives in a nursing home about an hour away, and I'm not sure if she would be able to figure out how to scan them and send them to me, but if it's important, I could drive out there and see if she can find them."

"Do you remember what the letters said?" Theresa asked, keeping her voice low. The movers were still carrying furniture from the truck into the building. "It doesn't need to be verbatim, just the general gist of it."

He frowned, thinking back. "They got two of them. One was before they accepted any offers on the building. It was one of those letters people sometimes send along with an offer, trying to convince the seller to accept their offer even if it isn't the highest. In this case, the person said something about how they had always loved the little brick building with the crooked door, how it wouldn't be just a business to them but a piece of history. They promised to take care of it and make sure it remained a cornerstone of Crooked Bay's downtown area for decades to come. My parents went with a higher offer since the building was part of their investment plan for their retirement. They got a second letter not long after they accepted the other offer. They weren't completely sure it was from the same person—this one was printed out instead of handwritten—but it was threatening. Whoever wrote it told them to rescind their acceptance of the other offer or they would be sorry. I don't remember if they went to the police or not. They were already in the process of moving out of town at that point, and I think nothing ever came of the threat."

"It has to be the same person," Theresa said. "Someone has wanted this building for a long time."

"I don't know exactly what you're going through, but it sounds unpleasant. Do you want me to see if my mother can find those letters?"

"If it's not too much trouble," Theresa said. "I'm not sure if they would help, but maybe it would get the police to take this more seriously. Out of curiosity, what sort of business did your parents have?"

"It was a little shake and burger place," he said. "It was closed for a couple of years before they sold the building." He gave the crêperie a fond smile. "I have a lot of good memories of this place. What are you turning it into?"

"A crêperie," she said. "If I had business cards,

I'd give you one. I'll be advertising in the weeks leading up to the grand opening. I really appreciate you coming out here despite my cousin's strange way of convincing you to do so. Stop by once we open, and there will be a free crêpe in it for you."

"I might just take you up on that offer," he said. "I hope I was of some help. If I do manage to get my hands on the letters, I'll let you know."

She thanked him again and watched for a few seconds as he walked away, then turned back to continue supervising the delivery of the furniture. It was a little reassuring to know that she, specifically, wasn't the one being targeted—whoever was doing this would have it out for anyone who bought the building. She just wished she knew who was behind it. Maybe it would be smarter to give up on the crêperie, but now that she had decided to do this, she was surprised by how much she wanted it.

Jace was right. She'd been a ghost for the last few years. She didn't want to go back to that.

CHAPTER NINE

Half an hour later, Theresa waved goodbye to the two kind men who had delivered her furniture and then shut and locked the crêperie's front door. She turned to look at the brand-new tables and chairs in the main room. The tables were round and big enough for four people to sit at. There was one large rectangular table at the back of the dining area for bigger parties. They were heavy, dark wood to match the floorboards. The chairs were black metal with cream colored cushions. It had been an expensive purchase, but she hoped they would last years. She walked through the room, occasionally straightening a chair or fixing a cushion into place. When she stood behind the counter and looked out across the dining area, she felt a surge of excitement. This was really happening. One day soon, people were going to be eating crêpes here—her crêpes.

After she checked on the desk in the office, the shelves she had purchased for supplies in the storage room, and the less fancy chairs, table, and padded stools she had bought for the kitchen and behind the counter, she checked her phone for the time. This was the only delivery for the day—the appliances would be coming later this week, along with much of the decor she had purchased online. She was still waiting on the security camera delivery too. According to the shipping company, they were supposed to arrive tomorrow.

There wasn't much else to do at the crêperie today, and she had the dinner with Clare tonight to prepare for. That was still half a day away, but she had a lot of shopping to do first. She'd been living mostly on takeout ever since she moved here, and it was time to stock up on groceries.

It was late afternoon by the time she got back to her apartment. She spent a couple of hours just relaxing on the couch, enjoying the gorgeous view of the bay. It wasn't as gray and rainy as it had been over the weekend, but there was still a strong, chilly wind. As she relaxed on the couch with a book in her hands and the lake just outside the window, she realized that despite all of the stress and worry around what was happening at the crêperie, she felt better than she had in years. She didn't feel like life was slowly grinding her down to nothing anymore. She owed her cousin and her son a thanks, it seemed. As long as she didn't end up getting murdered by the same person who had killed Levi Elwyn, that was.

She had just started preparing the ingredients for the crêpes when Clare arrived. She let her cousin in, told her to make herself at home, then returned to the kitchen. Clare came over to lean against the counter between the dining room and the kitchen. "Aren't crêpes breakfast food?" she asked, eyeing the ingredients skeptically. "You're mostly going to be open breakfast hours, right?"

"Breakfast and lunch," Theresa said. "I'm planning on closing at either two or three in the afternoon. I'm not sure which yet. I will be opening at seven, though. I'm hoping to be able to get some business from teenagers and parents who are dropping their kids off at school."

Clare wrinkled her nose. "You're going to be waking up ridiculously early. How many days a week are you going to be open?"

"Seven days a week, at least to begin with," Theresa said. "I know it sounds like a lot, and it will be. I'll be working there every day until I'm making enough to hire an employee or two. But I'll have every afternoon free, which should be nice."

She continued her cooking. She didn't have a flat griddle, so she was using a cast iron skillet. As she got closer to having the food ready, Clare set the table for them. Theresa had made two large crêpes, one savory and one sweet, and they split both of them between the two of them.

The savory crêpe had Canadian bacon, melted cheddar cheese, cream cheese, and green onions, and was topped by a small scoop of sour cream. The sweet one had a hazelnut spread with banana and whipped cream and a dusting of powdered sugar. Theresa watched as Clare tried each one, chewing slowly and wearing a serious expression on her face. Having taken a bite of both, she set her fork down and made a show of smacking her lips and considering what she was going to say.

"The sweet crêpes are called crêpe sucrées. The savory ones are crêpe salées. Now, come on, just tell me, Clare," Theresa said at last. "Are they terrible? Have Jace and Nicolas been lying to me for my whole life? Am I really the worst cook ever?"

"These are great," Clare said with a grin. "Seriously. Are these going to be on your menu to start with?"

"Yes, they're two of the six crêpes I'll be offering to start with. For the hazelnut one, I'll give people a choice between strawberries, bananas, or maraschino cherries. With the savory one, people can add eggs or tomatoes. I'm also going to have a chicken pesto savory crêpe and a vegetarian one with tomatoes, mozzarella, and fresh basil. I'll add more as time goes on, but I think you were right when you said I shouldn't start off with too much on the menu."

"I'm guessing this means you're still on the track to open the crêperie?" Clare asked.

"Yes. I'm not going to let this person scare me away." She hesitated. "Well, not unless things escalate a lot. By the way, thanks for sending Liam my way, but you could have been a bit less confusing when you told the poor man to come talk to me. He had no idea what it was I wanted from him at first."

"I have a reputation to keep up," Clare said. "I walk a fine line between being the town's eccentric psychic and being the town's weirdo. I've got to keep people talking about me to keep getting new clients. Besides, he came to see you, didn't he? It all worked out."

"Apparently, his parents got two letters—one

before they sold the building and one after. How did you find out they owned it, anyway?"

"I asked Martin. He delivered mail to them back when the place was a burger joint. He told me they had moved out of town, but their son was still around."

"Yeah, he said his mother, at least, lives in a nursing home about an hour from here. He didn't say anything about his father. I wonder if he passed away?"

"I've got no idea. I go to his bookstore sometimes, but I don't really know the guy. He didn't know who sent his parents those letters?"

Theresa shook her head. "No, but since it happened eight years ago, we can probably assume it wasn't teenagers. Whoever has been harassing the owners of my building is an adult. And they are serious about it. I think the person behind these threats is the same person who killed Levi."

"So, the wrong man is in jail?" Clare asked, putting her fork down. "You really think that?"

Theresa bit her lip. "I don't know the full story. I wasn't here when everything was happening. But it would make sense, right? Whoever is leaving these threats and vandalizing the building is obviously willing to go to extreme lengths to chase people away from it. For all we know, things with Levi escalated for years."

"I'm not saying you're wrong, but the guy they arrested… They found the murder weapon in the back seat of his car. Do you think that was a setup?"

"Maybe that guy was framed. And if that's the case, that means an innocent man is in prison. And that's just horrible. I'm half tempted to try to solve all of this myself just to get that poor man out from behind bars."

"Well, who do you think it is?" Clare asked. "It's got to be someone in town—probably someone I know. It's hard to imagine someone committing a murder and then just … going on with their lives like it never happened."

"Well, it has to be someone who's wanted the building for a long time. Maybe another business owner? I was talking to Alyson the other day when Jace was over, and she said there is one company that owns a lot of the commercial buildings in town, and the others rarely go up for sale. Maybe the killer is trying to chase me out like they chased Levi out so they can make an offer on this building when it goes up for sale at a lower price."

"You think Alyson has something to do with this?"

"Not her specifically, but I'm not going to cross her name off my mental list of suspects yet either," Theresa said. "You're the one who knows everyone in town. Who do you think it could be?"

Clare took another bite of her crêpe as she thought, a deep frown pulling down the corners of her mouth. "Well, Dora from the deli did mention she was thinking of putting a bid in on the building when it first came up for sale. I don't know if anything came of it, but maybe we could talk to her. I can't imagine her being a killer either, but I guess that's how it goes a lot of the time."

"Dora? The woman who owns Club King?"

Clare nodded. "She said something about wanting to move the deli to a building without an apartment upstairs. Maybe we should do some poking around."

CHAPTER TEN

The next morning, Theresa woke up to a notification that her security cameras were going to be delivered at some point that day. The email didn't say when they would get there, so she decided to spend most of the day at the crêperie. She had a few things she had to deal with on the legal side of opening a restaurant, but she could do that in town just as well as she could at her apartment. She packed up her laptop, made herself a cup of coffee to go, grabbed a yogurt from the fridge, and headed out.

It was a routine she had gone through a thousand times before in her life, but instead of driving to a dreary office building and taking an elevator down to the windowless basement, she stepped into her own little restaurant that was slowly starting to come together. She turned on the radio she had purchased a couple of days ago when she stopped by the hardware store to buy a ladder. While listening to quiet instrumental music as she checked through her emails, she made a few calls to make sure she was on track to open soon.

She was really getting down to the wire with choosing a name. She looked around the crêperie, hoping for inspiration, but nothing seemed to fit. The traits she loved about the building—the brick walls, the hardwood floors, how it was a little separate and smaller from the other buildings downtown—didn't really make for good names. No one was going to want to eat at a place called the Brick Crêpe.

She spent a quiet morning coming up with ever more ridiculous names and chasing down the last few bits of paperwork she had to turn in before she was ready to open. Before she knew it, it was time to meet Clare for lunch at Club King. Meeting her cousin for lunch or dinner was quickly becoming a new habit, but today they had another motive for going out to eat. They were going to play detective.

Clare was already there, leaning on the hood of her old convertible and texting on her phone until she spotted Theresa approaching and waved. They walked into the deli together. Dora wasn't behind the counter, but a quick check around the room showed that she was in conversation with an elderly couple at a table against the far wall. Clare and Theresa put in their lunch order with the employee at the counter, who rang them up, then found their usual table by the window. Theresa arranged herself so she could see the crêperie from where she was. She didn't want to miss the security camera delivery and have someone—namely, the person behind the vandalism and the threat—steal the box.

"Nice weather today," Dora said, approaching them once she had finished talking to her other customers. "It's finally warming up. I think I might leave a little early today to spend some time at the beach. Do the two of you have any fun plans this week?"

"I'm just going to be working on the crêperie," Theresa said, watching Dora's face closely for any sign of anger or jealousy. Dora just nodded and raised an eyebrow at Clare.

"I'll be working too," Clare said, wrinkling her nose. "The changing of the seasons is a time of great change for everyone, which means I have to commune with the powers that be more often. Speaking of, do you still think you might move Club King to a different location? I mentioned to Theresa that you had put an offer in on her building too. The two of us were wondering if you wanted us to keep an eye out for a promising new location."

Theresa shot Clare a panicked look. Why did her cousin think it was a good idea to give up their entire hand in one sentence?

"I'm actually glad my offer didn't get accepted," Doris said, giving Theresa an embarrassed smile. "I don't want you to think there's any hard feelings between us—the opposite, really. The tenants I was having an issue with moved out last month, and we're using the money we saved to start doing a pop-up stand at the high school and middle school once a week. If those go well, we might expand to surrounding areas. All in all, it's probably a good thing you got the place instead of us."

"I'm glad you found a solution that works for you," Theresa said. "The pop-up stand is a great idea. I bet the kids will be happy to have a tastier alternative than school lunches."

A bell on the counter dinged, and Dora turned to look in that direction. "It looks like your order is done —I'll go bring it over for you and then I'm going to take off." She winked at Theresa. "That's one of the benefits of being your own boss, you can take an afternoon off to go walk along the beach if you want to."

After Dora left, Theresa and Clare ate their lunch, talking about the encounter in hushed voices. They both agreed that it didn't seem as though Dora had a good reason to try to sabotage the crêperie, but Theresa didn't want to cross her off of her list yet. There might be something they were missing.

As she was finishing her sandwich, a delivery truck pulled up in front of the crêperie. She perked up, watching it. When it drove away, she was just able to make out a cardboard box sitting in front of the crêperie's door.

"It looks like my security cameras arrived," Theresa said. A second later, her phone dinged with an email confirming it.

"Well, I've got another hour before I've got to head off to meet a client. Do you want me to help you get started setting them up?"

"I would appreciate that. I'm not terrible with technology, but I'm really not the best either."

They threw their trash away and stepped out of the deli. Clare decided to leave her car where it was and walk back to get it when she had to go to work. As they walked down the sidewalk toward the intersection where they could cross the street, they passed Ridiculous Beans, and Clare paused.

"Do you mind if we stop for some coffee? Now that I'm full, I'm kind of getting tired. I could use a burst of energy to get through the rest of the day."

"Sure." She had already had a cup of coffee that morning, but a little bit more caffeine had never hurt anyone. Probably.

Alyson was the only one at the counter today. There were a couple of people in line, so they had to wait a few minutes before it was time for them to order. Alyson looked stressed as she took their orders, but no one else came in after them, and she relaxed slightly as she started making the drinks.

"We really need to hire another employee," she confided as she handed Clare her drink. "My shift was supposed to end half an hour ago, but my normal afternoon worker is late. I am at the end of my rope, I swear. Let me know if you know anyone who's willing to work for minimum wage. Unfortunately, that's all we can afford right now."

"Maybe a high school kid looking for some extra money?" Clare suggested.

Alyson wrinkled her nose. "That would be great if the hours I need covered weren't school hours. Anyway, enough complaining on my part. How are you two doing? You're getting to be a familiar face around here, Theresa. How are you liking Crooked Bay?"

"It's nice enough so far," Theresa said, watching as Alyson filled the top quarter of her cup with foamy whipped cream. "I'm starting to worry some people are upset I bought the building."

Alyson let out a quiet snort and handed her the cup. "Let me guess, Martin and his historical club?"

Theresa raised her eyebrows. She had been fishing to see if Alyson had a suspicious reaction to her words, but she hadn't expected her to mention the mailman.

"Well, I have seen Martin almost every day, but to be fair, that's his job. What's this about a historical club?"

"Oh, you don't know? Martin is president of the local historical society. They've been wanting to open a small museum about Crooked Bay. I think he had been hoping to purchase your building, but of course, that fell through. It's one of the older buildings downtown, you know."

"I see. He hasn't said anything to me about it."

"Well, I doubt he has a reason to. You bought the place, and it doesn't seem like you're moving anytime soon." The bell over the door jingled, and she glanced toward it. "Well, there's my employee. Better late than never, I guess. You two have a good evening."

Alyson walked over to her employee, already taking off her apron, Theresa and Clare left the coffee shop at the sounds of her berating the younger man behind them.

"She's not in a great mood today," Clare said. "That's good for me, at least—she always schedules readings when she's stressed."

"What exactly goes on during these psychic readings?" Theresa asked as they walked down to the intersection and waited for the light to change so they could walk across the street.

Clare grinned at her. "You can find out if you schedule one. I charge eighty bucks an hour. Sorry, no family discounts."

"Don't you still owe me almost two thousand dollars from that time I bought you a plane ticket when you were in Europe and your wallet got stolen?"

Clare's grin faded. "Well, maybe I can do a *small* family discount…"

CHAPTER ELEVEN

They had only gotten as far as unpacking the security cameras and laying them out on the big table in the dining room before Clare said she had to go. "I can come back this evening to help if you need it, though."

"I might," Theresa admitted. She looked down at the various wires, screws, and the box that would record the footage. She knew she could figure it out if she tried hard enough, but she wasn't sure if it wouldn't just be easier to hire someone to come and do it. The only downside to that was that she would need to wait at least a few more days before they could fit her into their schedule.

She waved goodbye to her cousin as she walked across the street and down the road to where her car was parked. It was a cloudless day, and there was a warm breeze coming off the lake. She would much rather be spending her time outside than in here, poking away at the cameras, but she really wanted to get at least one set up. She didn't know when the person who had been harassing her might come back, and she didn't want to miss her chance to catch them on tape.

She turned to go back inside when she spotted a familiar figure coming down the sidewalk: Martin. She waved at the mailman, and he nodded back, coming over and handing her a few pieces of mail. All of it looked like junk mail, but she thanked him anyway.

"I hate to be a bother, but would it be possible for me to come in and use your restroom? I've been drinking more water with this nicer weather, and, well, it went right through me."

"Of course," she said, stepping aside so he could go in through the front door. She'd responded automatically, but as soon as the words were out of her mouth, she regretted them. She remembered what Alyson had said earlier. Martin was someone who had wanted this building. He was certainly old enough to have put in an offer on it back when Liam's parents had sold it. She eyed him as he walked toward the back and decided to stay near the front door and pretend like she was looking through her mail. If he tried something, escape would only be a few steps away.

She heard a door open and close, then open again, and saw him coming out of the kitchen, not the bathroom. She opened her mouth to point out where the correct room was, but he seemed to have spotted it and made his way over. It wasn't long before she heard the toilet flush and he was on his way out.

"Sorry about that. It's been a while since I've been in here, and I got a bit turned around. I think I about gave that poor woman a heart attack." He chuckled.

Theresa had been all set to say, *It's no problem, have a nice day,* but her mouth worked in silent shock instead. "Woman? What woman?"

Martin gave her a strange look. "Whoever's helping you in the kitchen. I surprised her when I went back there. Thanks for letting me use your restroom, ma'am. I appreciate it."

He let himself out through the front door, leaving Theresa to stare after him. Slowly, her gaze drifted back to the kitchen.

Had Clare come back? No—why would her

cousin go in through the back and not through the front? Was Martin imagining things?

Slowly, quietly, she set the mail down on a table and walked toward the kitchen door. Her heart was in her throat. Somewhere in the back of her mind, she knew she should call the police, but she had to see for herself. Who was back there, *if* there was even anyone back there in the first place. She was certain she had locked the back entrance, though she didn't remember the last time she had used it.

Ever so quietly, she pushed open the kitchen door and peered inside. The kitchen looked empty, just like it should be. The back door was shut, and nothing seemed out of place. Maybe Martin really had imagined it.

"Hello?" she said, her voice loud in the quiet building. She stepped through the door and let it close behind her. "Is anyone in here?"

She was half expecting someone to push their way out of one of the cupboards under the long counter. What she wasn't expecting was to hear the shifting of fabric behind her and feel the cold prick of a blade press against the back of her neck. The intruder hadn't been hiding in a cupboard. She had been hiding behind the door.

CHAPTER TWELVE

Theresa didn't dare move. She was surprised her heart hadn't stopped beating, she was standing so still. It felt as if she could barely even think. Her brain just kept repeating the fact that someone was holding a knife to the back of her neck over and over again. Maybe it wasn't quite as frightening as if they'd held it to her jugular, but she had no doubt whoever was standing behind her was the same person who had killed Levi. And they had killed him by stabbing him in the back. It was safe to assume whoever held that knife knew what they were doing with it.

"I warned you." The voice came out low, as if the speaker was trying to change it so she wouldn't be recognized, but it was definitely a woman's voice. "I didn't want to hurt anyone else. I tried to get you to leave without doing this. Why did you have to swoop in and buy this place up? It would've been mine if it wasn't for you."

"Who are you?" Theresa asked. The voice was familiar, but she couldn't quite place it.

"Someone who is tired of always coming in last. Hold out your hand." Puzzled, Theresa did as she was told. "Not like that. To your side. I'm going to put something in your palm."

She felt the brush of fingers on her skin and looked down to see a handful of small pills lying in the palm of her hand. The knife pricked her neck.

"Don't look around. Keep looking forward. Swallow the pills."

"I'm not doing that."

"Swallow them." The pressure of the knife on the back of her neck increased. She wondered if she was bleeding where the tip was poking her. Still, there was no way she was swallowing whatever that medication was. Before she could reconsider her actions, she threw the pills across the room, where they tumbled away on the tiles. The woman behind her let out a wordless sound of irritation.

"You'll go to sleep, and you won't wake up. It's not a bad way to die. I can't have this look like another murder, or the police will be out looking for me. Go pick the pills up."

In her annoyance, the woman had forgotten to modulate her voice. With a creeping sense of horror, Theresa recognized it.

"Alyson?"

The knife poked her even harder, and she winced. "Shut up. Just shut up. I *have to* kill you now, do you understand that? None of this went the way it was supposed to."

"I don't understand. You want this building?"

"Of course I do," Alyson said. "You know what price it was listed at. There's never going to be another building this affordable in town again. You've seen my current coffee shop. The ceiling is leaking, rent is ridiculously high, and I can barely make ends meet. This place was supposed to be mine, give me a fresh start. It would have been, if it wasn't for you."

"You killed Levi, didn't you? Why?" It didn't make sense to her, to kill over a building or a business. Work was important, of course, but it was nothing compared to a human life.

"Think about what sort of business he had here," Alyson said, her voice quiet. "I'm sure you at least looked that much up. It was a coffee shop. I can barely make ends meet as the only coffee shop in town. I tried to buy this building when it originally sold eight years ago. He snatched it out from under me and opened a coffee shop that was my direct competitor. He was putting me out of business. I tried to convince him to change the focus of his business, to move to a different town, anything. He refused to budge." She took a deep breath. Her words came out faster, as if they had been weighing on her for a long time. "I didn't plan it. One day I just snapped. He had been opening some plastic bags with a knife, and he set the knife on the counter and turned around. It was in my hand before I had a chance to think about what I was doing. I don't regret it. When I saw the price it was being sold at, I was certain it was mine this time, but then some out-of-town buyer offered asking price and got it." The knife traced a cold line down her neck. "I bet the price would be even lower with two deaths here. But I already pinned the first murder on someone else. I can't make it obvious what happened here, or the police will never stop looking for me. That's why I need you to take those pills. It will be a peaceful death, I promise. I've heard a lot about you from Clare. Your husband died three years ago. Don't you want to join him? It won't be so bad. Just like falling asleep."

"You're insane," Theresa said. "Put the knife

down. We can figure something out."

"We're past—" Alyson broke off at the sound of a male voice calling out in the dining room. Theresa hadn't installed a bell above the door yet, so neither of them had heard someone coming in.

"Hello? Is anyone here?"

She hadn't been expecting anyone, and had no idea who he was, but she wasn't about to waste this chance. She stumbled forward, away from Alyson and the knife, and at the same time called out, "I'm in here! Help me!"

Alyson swore and lurched toward her. Now that Theresa could see her, she saw that the woman looked more stressed than ever, and absolutely deranged. She might have felt pity for the other woman if she hadn't already killed one person and threatened to kill her.

Theresa dodged out of the way, then ran over to the tall ladder she and Clare had leaned against the wall in the kitchen in case they needed it for the windows again. She pushed it over onto Alyson with a clang, and the woman went down beneath it, struggling to get the unwieldy aluminum frame off of herself. The kitchen door opened, and Theresa saw Liam, the bookshop owner, staring in with wide eyes. He had two papers clenched in his hand.

"I … I got those letters you wanted. What's going on?"

"Thanks for the letters," Theresa said, breathing hard. "I'm sure the police will want them. This is the woman who wrote them."

EPILOGUE

The grand opening happened on a warm spring day. The sun was shining, there were a few white, fluffy clouds far up in the sky, and a breeze was coming in off the bay. The crêperie windows had been repaired, and Theresa knew the little building was as ready for its new life as it was going to get.

"Five minutes, Mom."

Jace and Layla had both come to help for the day. The same evening Alyson was arrested, Theresa had finally told her son everything that was going on. He had been upset at first that she had kept it from him, but things were finally back to normal between them, for the most part. She still couldn't quite believe that her son, her little boy, was engaged, but seeing him and Layla work together today to put the finishing touches on the crêperie and help her get ready for her grand opening had reassured her that he knew what he was doing. She might not know Layla that well yet, but it was obvious her son did, and that he was confident the decision to spend the rest of his life with her had been the right one.

"What if no one shows up?" Theresa asked. It was an absurd thing to say—Clare had already reported that there were a few people waiting in line outside, but she'd had a recurring nightmare every day for the past week that she never got a single customer at the crêperie and ended up shutting it down after a month without any visitors at all.

"Don't be silly, my clients trust me too much for that to happen," Clare said. She was on drink duty. It was her job to manage the expensive espresso machine and fetch people drinks from the refrigerator when they wanted them.

"What do you mean by that?"

"Nothing, nothing," Clare said. She stepped back from the drink fridge to admire her organizational skills.

"No, really, what do you mean by that, Clare?" Theresa asked. She was beginning to worry her cousin had something up her sleeve.

"Just that I've been telling my clients the powers

that be want them to come here. I even slipped one of those coupons for twenty percent off their first order into my tarot deck to help push them into it."

"You abuse your powers horribly, you know that?"

"I can promise you not a single person is going to walk out of here today without a smile on their face. They will be better off for coming here, and you'll be better off for it too. Now, quit worrying. How long do we have, Jace?"

"Two minutes left." He was in charge of keeping the fresh ingredients prepared so they didn't run out. After today, Theresa would be doing all of this herself until she got around to hiring an employee, but she was expecting to be busier than usual on the first day.

"All right, places, everyone," Theresa said. "Jace, keep working on those green onions. We're going to need a lot of them. Clare, no weird psychic stuff today. And Layla... Well, I don't think I need to tell you anything. You're good to go at the register?"

Layla nodded. "It's just like the one I used at my college job. I've got this."

Theresa took a deep breath. "And you guys think the name is okay?"

"It's perfect, Terra," Clare said. "Now, put a smile on your face. You look like you're about to faint."

"It's time, Mom. Seven in the morning. I can't believe I'm actually awake this early."

Theresa approached the front door, unlocked it, and pulled it open. A bell jingled cheerfully above her head. She took a deep breath and smiled at the people waiting outside.

"Hi, everyone. Welcome to the Crooked Crêperie. We're open for business."